Dedicated to the children of the barrios who live far away from the Caribbean magic that weaves the stories of this book.

the Song of el Coqui

and other tales of Puerto Rico

Nicholasa Mohr
and Antonio Martorell

VIKING

VIKING
Published by the Penguin Group
Penguin Books USA Inc., 375 Hudson Street, New York, New York 10014, U.S.A.
Penguin Books Ltd, 27 Wrights Lane, London W8 5TZ, England
Penguin Books Australia Ltd, Ringwood, Victoria, Australia
Penguin Books Canada Ltd, 10 Alcorn Avenue, Toronto, Ontario, Canada M4V 3B2
Penguin Books (N.Z.) Ltd, 182–190 Wairau Road, Auckland 10, New Zealand

Penguin Books Ltd, Registered Offices: Harmondsworth, Middlesex, England

First published in 1995 by Viking, a division of Penguin Books USA Inc.

1 3 5 7 9 10 8 6 4 2

LIBRARY OF CONGRESS CATALOGING-IN-PUBLICATION DATA
Mohr, Nicholasa.
The song of el coquí and other tales of Puerto Rico / Nicholasa Mohr and Antonio Martorell.   p.   cm.
Summary: A collection of three folktales which reflect the diverse heritage within the Puerto Rican culture.
ISBN 0-670-85837-4
1. Tales—Puerto Rico. [1. Folklore—Puerto Rico.] I. Martorell, Antonio, ill. II. Title.
PZ8.1.M72So 1995 398.2'0972950452—dc20 [E] 94-43075 CIP AC

Printed in Singapore
Set in Caxton Bold

Introduction

All three tales in this book have been written with affection and respect for the rich and complex ancestral traditions that make up Puerto Rican culture. The history, the characters, and the elements depicted are all part of the mixed heritage of Latin America, drawn predominantly from the indigenous inhabitants, the Africans, and the Spaniards. The stories told here are especially representative of the Spanish Caribbean, and in particular, the island of Puerto Rico.

Each animal in these stories exemplifies one of the three most important cultural groups in Puerto Rico. The tiny coquí represents the indigenous Tainos, inhabitants who worshiped the great god Huracán. La Guinea, the guinea hen, is symbolic of the African peoples who were brought in as captive slaves and subsequently have had an indelible impact on the culture of Puerto Rico. The story of La Mula, the mule, is a parable about the Spaniards who conquered the island by force and eventually merged with the rest of the population to create the culture of the island of Puerto Rico as we know it today.

Together these stories have been woven into the colorful and luxuriant tapestry that is the essence of Puerto Rican folklore.

the Song of el Coqui

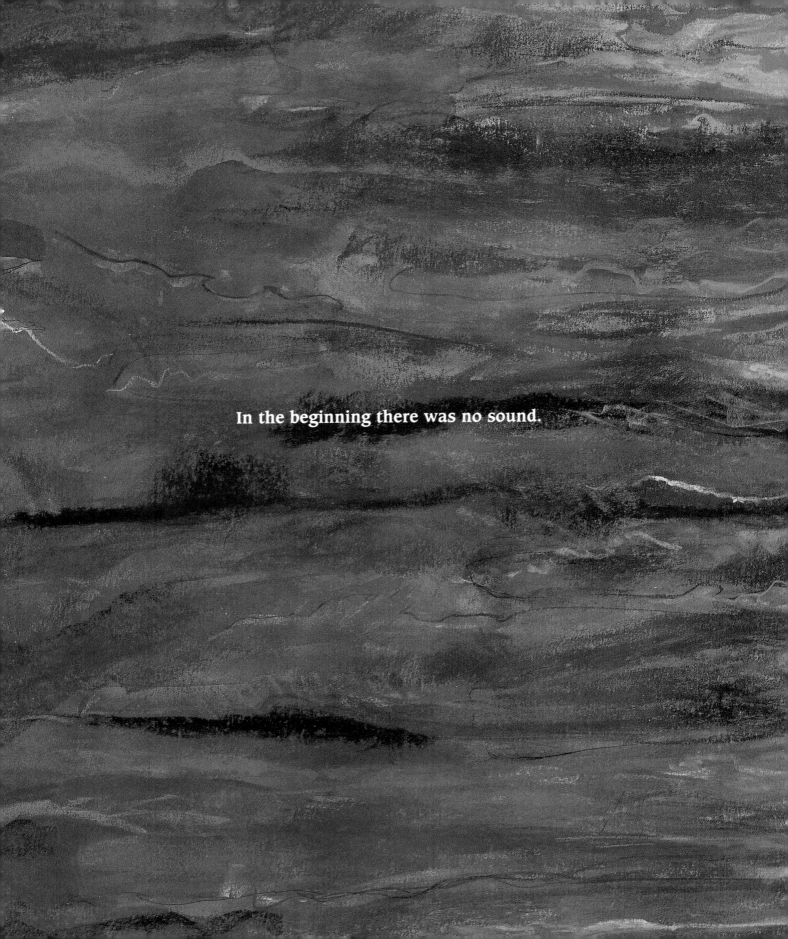

In the beginning there was no sound.

Then grass grew, trees appeared, flowers blossomed, and the wind whispered through the mountains. A hush floated along the breeze. The god Huracán smiled down from the highest mountain peak, enjoying his home, the beautiful island of Borinquén.

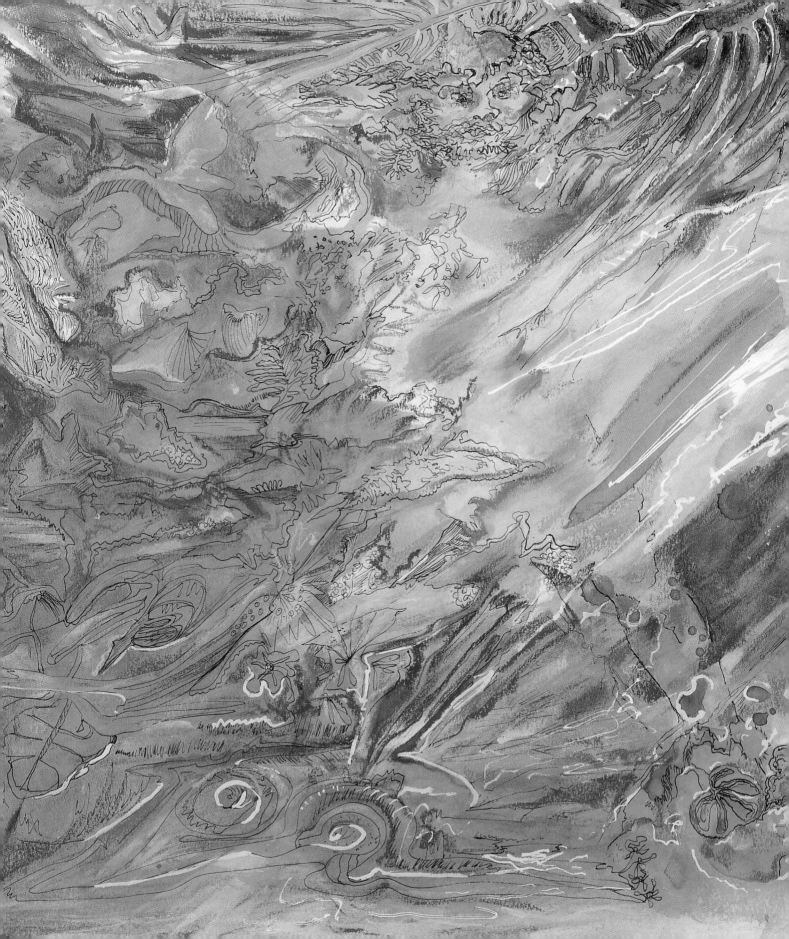

One day Huracán looked down from his mountain and felt sad. There was no music to make him happy. So the great Huracán made a storm. Rain, thunder, and lightning struck the land for the next million years.

After the storm, silence reigned once more. Not even the wind could break the stillness. Huracán became furious. He cursed the silence that surrounded him. Exhausted from making such a long storm, he fell into a deep sleep.

A sound . . . at first like a raindrop . . . woke Huracán. He stood, stretched, and listened. The sound grew louder and louder. It echoed once, it echoed twice. Soon the sound was everywhere . . . *Coquí, coquí,* it sang. In the rivers, through the forests, in the flowers, in the palm trees, in the caves, even in the wind . . . *Coquí, coquí, coquí,* it sang. Huracán looked everywhere. He searched high up in the mountains and way down in the valleys. Yet he could not find where the sound came from.

He continued his search, traveling to the farthest regions and back. At last the god Huracán could move no more. Tired and hungry, he stopped by a mango tree. As he reached for a ripe, juicy fruit, Huracán felt a heavy dewdrop fall into his palm. The tiniest frog stared up at him. *Coquí, coquí,* it sang. *Coquí, coquí,* the song echoed everywhere. Tiny frogs perched on leaves, on blades of grass, and on the petals of flowers, echoing the song. Huracán laughed with pleasure. "Coquí, coquí," he sang, and was no longer sad.

Swiftly, all the animals on the island began to sing along with the chorus of

*coquí*s. Soon the god Huracán heard the refrain of the nightingale and the buzzing of the bees and the hooting of the owls. And from the sea, the song of dolphins joined the song of the coquí.

To this day all the animals on the island of Borinquén sing happily, each in its own voice. Yet none echoes as loud and as sweet as the song of the tiny coquí.

La

Guinea

the stowaway hen

In La Guinea's small village on the coast of West Africa, shots rang out. Slave traders had raided her home. People screamed and fled for their lives. La Guinea ran around wildly, dodging bullets. She hid in a basket where she was safe. La Guinea waited for the fighting to cease. Hours passed, until she finally fell fast asleep.

A fierce rocking motion awoke her. Cackling loudly, she jumped out of the basket—but darkness surrounded her. "Help! Help!" she cackled wildly. No one answered. *Swish, swish,* she heard. La Guinea was hungry and thirsty. She searched among the many sacks until she found some grain. She ate heartily and drank from a vat of water. When she heard footsteps, La Guinea hid in her basket.

Day after day lightness appeared and disappeared,
until one day the rocking stopped. She was
carried away, inside the basket, and set
on firm ground.

La Guinea peeked out to see the docks of Ponce harbor. Horses and carriages sped by, and throngs of people were everywhere. Swiftly she leapt out and scampered toward the large plaza. "Where am I? What is this place?" she cackled.

People stared in amazement. "What is that?" "Is it a hen?" "I think it's a giant pigeon!" they shouted.

"Let's get her!" screamed a policeman. And they set out to capture her.

But La Guinea flapped her wings, flew up, and perched herself on a tree limb. "Get away . . . get away . . . get away!" she warned. A young boy climbed up and reached out across the branches. Frightened, she flew across and landed on top of a large statue.

"She's a strange and evil bird! A bad omen!" yelled the townspeople. "Let's kill her!" They all began pelting her with rocks.

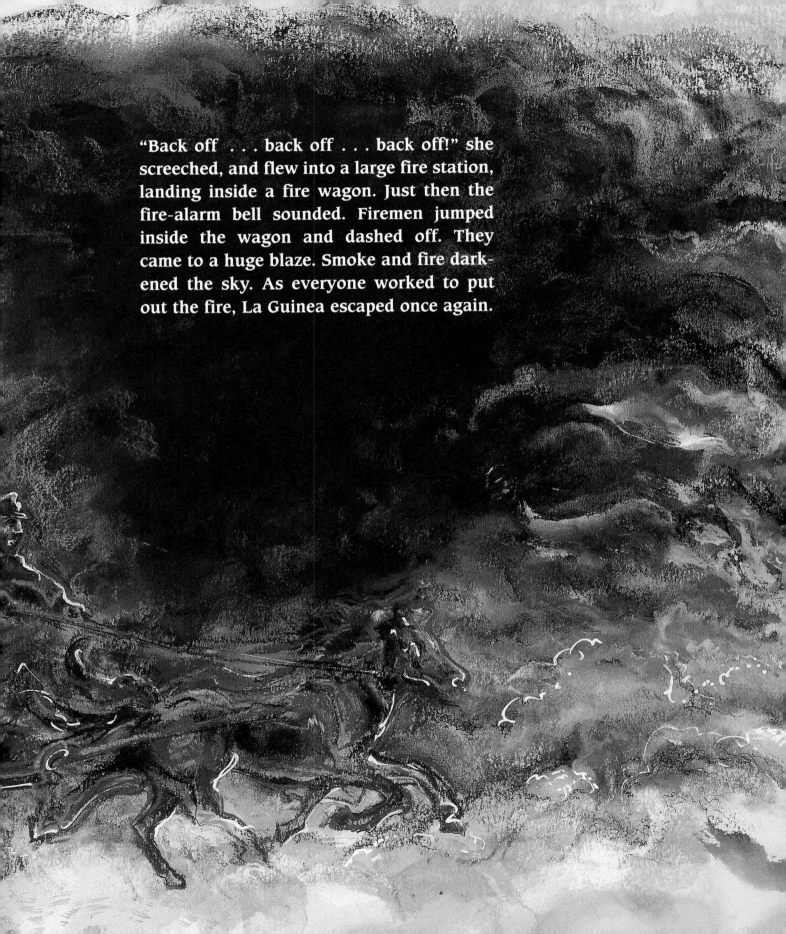

"Back off . . . back off . . . back off!" she screeched, and flew into a large fire station, landing inside a fire wagon. Just then the fire-alarm bell sounded. Firemen jumped inside the wagon and dashed off. They came to a huge blaze. Smoke and fire darkened the sky. As everyone worked to put out the fire, La Guinea escaped once again.

She found a *batey* and decided to rest herself.

Inside the cabin Don Elías the mask-maker was working. As he glanced out of his window he caught sight of La Guinea. "Why, that is the most interesting bird I have ever seen," he said. "I will keep her here and give her a good home." The mask-maker brought her some bread crumbs and fresh water. It was the first friendly gesture she had received. La Guinea ate and drank until she was full. At last she had found a good home. La Guinea's striking features inspired Don Elías as he made his masks.

Although she made friends with all the other animals, as the weeks passed La Guinea became lonely. No one else looked like her. She wished she could have a mate as the others did. One sunny morning La Guinea sat thinking that she was fated to live without a mate, when suddenly, she heard a familiar sound. There before her stood her master holding a cage. Inside was a guinea cock—as handsome a bird as she had ever seen.

For many years thereafter, La Guinea and her family inspired the kind Don Elías to create beautiful masks. His masks became popular on the island of Puerto Rico and brought him fame and fortune.

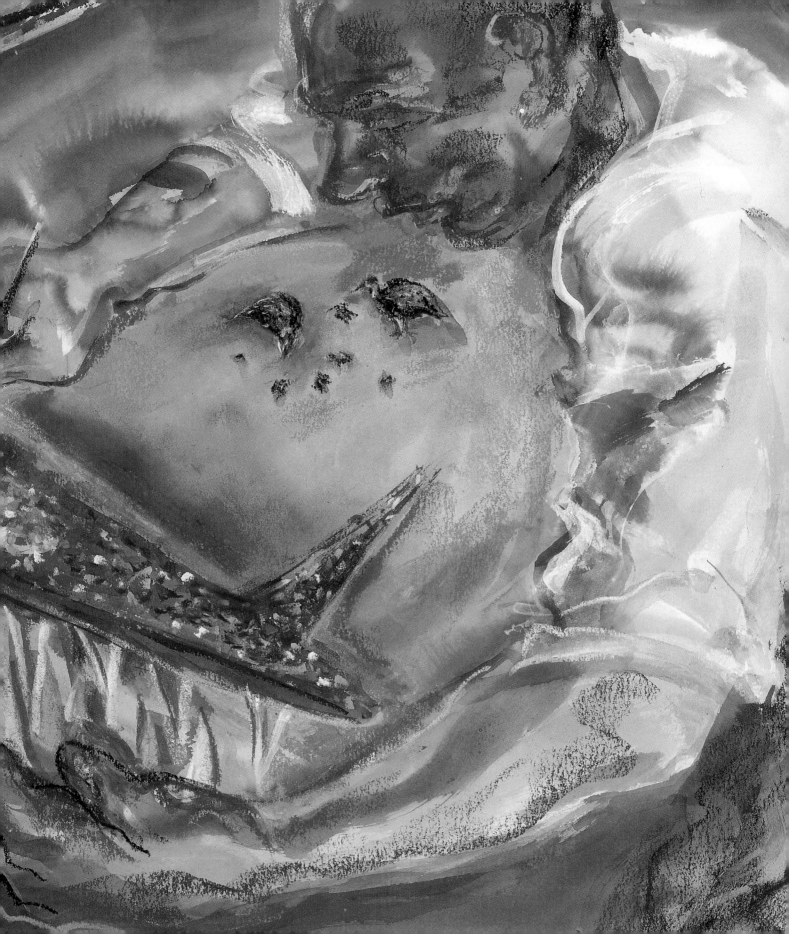

Bandits shoved La Mula, hurrying her along the mountainous path. La Mula groaned as she carried the heavy sacks of grain and barrels of wine along the narrow trail. "Go on, you lazy mule!" the bandits shouted, and whipped her. They pushed her so hard she lost her footing and almost plunged down the sharp ravine. "Watch your step, mule, or we'll skin you alive!" She traveled without rest and with little food, only grazing along the roadside for nourishment.

Weeks passed, until the bandits finally reached the port of Cádiz in southern Spain. The wicked bandits sold the contraband. "The mule's included for a few more coins," they bargained.

On board ship La Mula rested herself and licked her wounds. At night she wondered where she was going. Who would be her next masters? Would they treat her kindly? La Mula sighed. Only time would tell.

At the docks of San Juan harbor, La Mula was taken to the marketplace. There, barrels of olives, crates of salted codfish, leather saddles, and other goods from the ship were being sold. La Mula was also sold to the highest bidder.

"Come with me, you stubborn mule!" bellowed Don Eduardo, the road engineer. La Mula trembled when she heard his mean voice. As her new master, Don Eduardo worked La Mula long hours and gave her little food. She labored alongside the slaves, who were treated no better.

From sunrise to sundown, La Mula and the slaves toiled, clearing and building the roads. One day when she was hardly able to stand, La Mula cried for help. "Help me . . . please give me water," she brayed. The workers ignored her, but one slave, Otilio, offered her a cool drink.

"Here my friend," he told her. "Since we both work like mules, let me share my water." Otilio also shared his lunch. Soon they became friends.

"Why, that slave Otilio gets more work from that stubborn mule than I do," said Don

Eduardo. "I'll pair them and make them work even harder."

But Otilio had confided in La Mula. "I am planning our escape," he said. "We will go up into the hills where my people, Los Cimarrones, are. We were all once slaves who ran away. My people are proud and they are free. A year ago I was captured when I left my village to hunt for meat. But once we return we will live in freedom, too." The following week in the dark of night, they fled the wretched work camp.

During the day, Otilio and La Mula hid in caves, avoiding search parties. They traveled only at night. In the dark and dense steep woods, Otilio mounted La Mula. "You must be my eyes and guide our steps Mula," whispered Otilio. "If you fail and they capture us we will both die."

"I will not fail you, master," she softly brayed. La Mula used her talent for climbing and crept up snakelike trails. She strode by the vertical cliffs, taking only the right number of steps along the cramped slopes to avoid toppling to a sure death. With each passing night, they got farther and farther away from their enemies, until one day Otilio shouted, "We're home, Mula!" and pointed to his village.

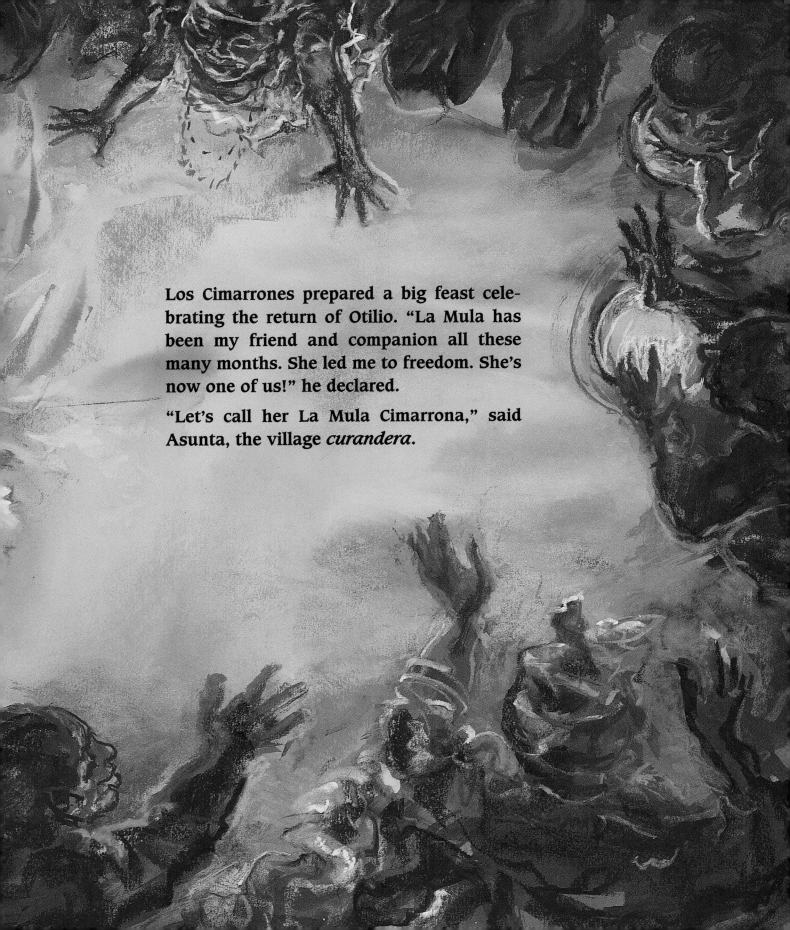

Los Cimarrones prepared a big feast celebrating the return of Otilio. "La Mula has been my friend and companion all these many months. She led me to freedom. She's now one of us!" he declared.

"Let's call her La Mula Cimarrona," said Asunta, the village *curandera*.

In the years that followed, other slaves escaped and joined Los Cimarrones. La Mula Cimarrona carried water and food; worked to build *bohios* and *bateys*. She lived a long, happy, and fruitful life.

To this day she continues to be revered and remembered as La Mula Cimarrona, who helped to expand a Cimarron village of free people on the island of Puerto Rico.

A few facts about these stories:

The tiny frog *el coquí* survives only in Puerto Rico. It was named after the loud sound it makes—*coquí*—which is heard all over the island.

The island of Puerto Rico was named *Borinquén* by the Tainos, original inhabitants of the island. The Tainos worshiped the god *Huracán*, who they believed was the creator of thunder, lightning, and horrendous storms.

La Guinea, the guinea fowl, originated in Africa and is believed to have been brought to the island of Puerto Rico during the time of the slave trade. The guinea fowl is independent by nature and difficult to subdue, and when threatened it will emit a blaring cackle.

El Batey is a front yard, primarily found in rural areas, made of solidly packed down earth. It is a Taino word that has been adapted into the Puerto Rican vocabulary.

La Mula, the mule, is a crossbreed between a donkey and a horse. In Spanish it is referred to as "she." The mule was brought in by the Spaniards and used for heavy labor, such as building roads through the rough, mountainous terrain.

Los Cimarrones, the Cimarrons, is a name given to the captive African slaves who escaped into the mountains and formed villages where they lived as free people.

El Bohio is a round cabin that used to be common in rural Puerto Rico. It was made of stalks or palm fronds, with a thatched roof.

La curandera, female, or *el curandero*, male, refers to a healer or a wise person of the village.